O9-BRY-582

A SAFE PLACE

EILEEN SPINELLI

CALLED HOME

illustrated by CHRISTY HALE

MARSHALL CAVENDISH

NEW YORK

Marshall Cavendish, 99 White Plains Road, Tarrytown, NY 10591

Library of Congress Cataloging-in-Publication Data
Spinelli, Eileen.
   A safe place called home / by Eileen Spinelli; illustrated by
Christy Hale.
      p. cm.
   Summary: While walking home from school, a young boy experiences
many scary things, both imaginary and real, and looks forward to being
safe and snug at home with his parents.
   ISBN 0-7614-5085-8
   [1. Fear–Fiction. 2. Home–Fiction. 3. Security (Psychology)–Fiction.
4. Stories in rhyme.] I. Hale, Christy, ill. II. Title.
   PZ8.3.S759 Saf 2001   [E]–dc21   00-060378

The text of this book is set in 17.5/22 pt. Bell.
The illustrations are mixed media.
Printed in Italy

First edition

6   5   4   3   2   1

For those sweet, safe places called libraries,
especially the Chester County Public Library in Exton, Pennsylvania
and the Sellers Library in Upper Darby, Pennsylvania,
and to Miss Armstrong, wherever you may be.
—E. S.

For my niece,
Sarah Lau Hale
—C. H.

When the stray dog barks,
when the lightning sparks,
when a storm cloud follows me,

when the big kids shout
as they race about . . .
home is the place to be.

When the sirens blast
and the trucks roar past,
when I fall and scrape my knee,

when the tomcat yowls
and the bully scowls . . .
home is the place to be.

When the puddle's wide.
When I want to hide
from the shark I think I see,

when I hear a crash
near the bin for trash . . .
home is the place to be.

When the hawk swoops low,
when the snake glides slow,
when I'm chased by a bumblebee,

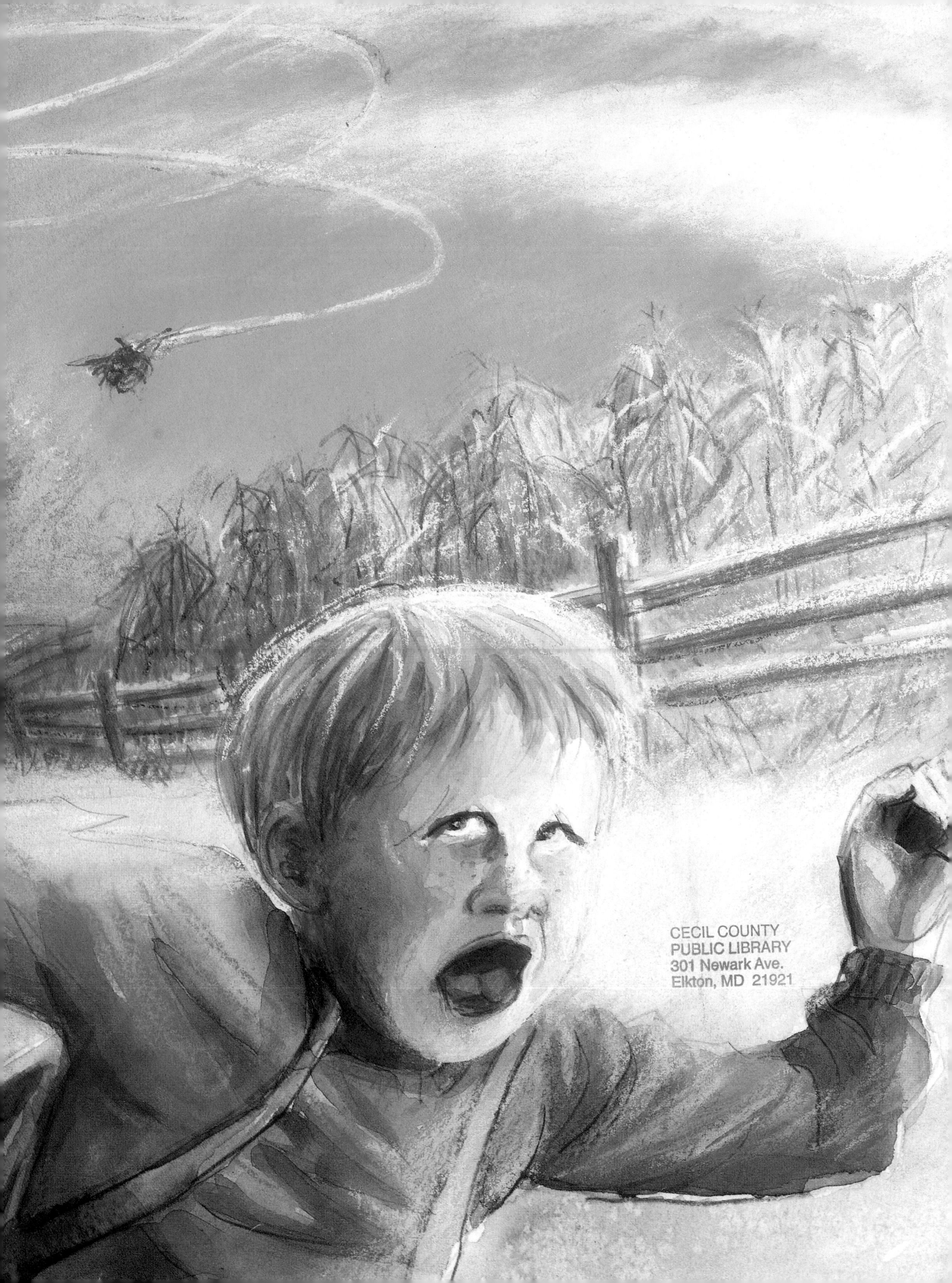

when the spider creeps,
when the bullfrog leaps . . .
home is the place to be.

When the dead leaves whirl
in a smoky swirl,
when the scarecrow grins with glee,

when the wash lines flap
and the shutters slap . . .
home is the place to be.

When it's late at night
and the bat takes flight
and the great owl leaves its tree,

when the pale moon peeks
and an old cart creaks . . .
home is the place to be.

Home is the place all safe and snug
when I'm scared as I can be
with Mommy's smile and Daddy's hug . . .
home is the place for me

for sure.
Home is the place for me.